BOUNCE BACK

by MISAKO ROCKS!

Feiwel and Friends
New York

A FEIWEL AND FRIENDS BOOK
An imprint of Macmillan Publishing Group, LLC
120 Broadway, New York, NY 10271
mackids.com

Library of Congress Control Number: 2021907139

First edition, 2021
Book design by Sharismar Rodriguez and Cindy De la Cruz

Feiwel and Friends logo designed by Filomena Tuosto
Printed in China by RR Donnelley Asia Printing Solutions Ltd.,
Dongguan City, Guangdong Province.

ISBN 978-1-250-76845-2 (hardcover)
10 9 8 7 6 5 4 3 2 1

ISBN 978-1-250-80629-1 (paperback)
10 9 8 7 6 5 4 3 2 1

This book is dedicated to any young person
out there who is struggling to find
their place in this world.

CHAPTER 1

SEVERAL MONTHS AGO, IN OSAKA, JAPAN

Hey, girls! Let's do shooting drills again. Finals are coming soon, and we can't waste any time!

Okay, Captain! Make two lines.

I know we're gonna win this year. I can feel it. It's our time!

I believe it! We've worked so hard and dominated our division this season!

2

3

4

Just like that, my life was turned upside down.

6

8

9

Whoa...This is like a movie! We're going to live in this city?

14

19

CHAPTER 2

25

26

27

Sugoi... Nala,

where did you find that dress?

Oh! I made it.

What?! **This** dress?

HAHAHA!!

Yeah. I always make my own clothes.

You should see her entire collection. It's going to blow your mind.

Hey, Lilico, can you ask your dad to show me his Japanese sword collection, too? Your dad is so cool.

My dad? Well, my parents think you are great.

ラー

Oh, Nala, I just remember, do you want to try on my school uniform from Japan? I have at home.

ラーメン

Really?! A REAL Japanese school uniform?! Is it like a sailor uniform? Oh my gosh, when can I try it on?

Oh boy...That was intense. It almost seems like Emma is meaner to Nala than she is to me!

Mom! Where's one of my Japanese school uniforms?

In my closet. Why do you need it?

I'm going to show it to Nala.

Okay. Let me look.

Here!

Thanks, Mom!

It looks like you guys have become good friends.

41

45

47

52

55

She started ignoring me and making fun of me in front of everybody.

What?! That's awful!

I know! She thinks she's better than everybody! You should stay away from her. Not worth it.

Anyway, let's talk later, okay?

Okay! See you...

PSST!

I understand what she's saying. But I disagree with her.

Nicco?! Were you spying on us?!

Look at them! They think you're a mouse!

CHAPTER 3

Oh... sorry!

Argh!!! Don't touch it!!!!!!

No, no. I'm sorry. I'm usually not like this! But if something happened to my wig collection, I don't know what I'd do... It's the most important thing in my life! When I wear them, I feel complete.

Y-yeah. I can see that.

I won't touch her wig collection...ever...again!

Hey, Nala. Thank you.

What do you mean?

Hey, you wanna do each other's hair? You've got such beautiful hair!

61

I hated school so much, especially after that thing with Emma and my basketball. But having you and Henry there for me, things have gotten so much better. I mean, my dad loves hanging out with Henry! So weird. But kind of cool, I guess.

Hahaha. Yeah, Henry is cool. And you're awesome, Lilico!

I know she still wants to play basketball! I have to do something about this.

63

67

71

73

74

76

CHAPTER 4

86

My mom always tries to make me take her class. But no way!

Yeah. My mom tried to get me to take it, too!

So, Lilico, you should try playing basketball in the gym tomorrow.

Tomorrow? What if the girls see me?

That's the point! Show them what you got!

Yeah! I don't know much about basketball, but you look awesome. Emma will be blown away. Do it, Lilico!

Listen to your friends.

Okay, if you say so.

91

92

93

94

98

They were watching me? Were they making fun of me again?

Wanna play one-on-one?

Sure. Let's do it.

116

117

118

CHAPTER 5

120

126

127

131

One, two, three, four...

...five, six, seven, eight!

Kiara? Are you okay?

What? I'm fine. Come on, let's finish up.

Is Kiara okay? It seems like maybe something is wrong.

Kiara, you don't have to push yourself if you don't feel good. Guys, can we take a break?

When we were in English class, she said she had a headache.

Really? Are you okay?

133

137

Wow. I never thought I'd find something in common with Emma! This is wild!

How was it? Did you have a good time?

Yeah! It was so great! It almost feels like Emma and I are becoming friends! She's actually fun. I'm so glad that I joined the team. Thank you, Nicco.

I'm so happy to see you like this. Good for you, Lilico!

143

145

151

BOOOOO!!!!

Miss! Miss! Miss! Miss!!!!

163

CHAPTER 6

173

177

188

189

We were laughing so hard, and Coach got mad. Connor ran away from him.

Hahahaha!

Argh. This is so weird. I can talk to him normally at school...Why can't we talk normally now?

No problem! How's the cake going? It smells amazing.

Henry, thank you for all the balloons! So kawaii!

We're almost done!

195

199

CHAPTER 7

Where's Nala...?

She's not at school!

Lilico!

Lilico, how are you feeling? We were worried about you since you didn't come to school the last couple of days.

Thank you. I'm okay.

Yeah. I didn't expect that at all.

Ready to go to practice?

Yep! Let's go!

Oh boy. I don't think I can bring up anything about Nala, otherwise Emma is going to flip out...

I have to go to Nala's house... I have to see her.

Why are you in such a hurry?

Uh...gotta go now. My mom keeps calling me for some reason. See you later!

See you!

219

CHAPTER 8

223

225

233

234

Hey, guys! Sorry I'm late...

I hope they'll agree to this!

You really need to talk to everyone. They feel betrayed.

Oh no... Okay.

Guys, can we talk a little bit?

235

237

238

BOUNCE BACK FASHION DIY
BY NALA!

LILICO: 13 Years Old
HEIGHT: 5'3"
HOMETOWN: Osaka, Japan
ZODIAC SIGN: Aries
FAVORITE FOOD: Tonkatsu!

FASHION DIY: LILICO!

1. FIND A PLAIN T-SHIRT.

2. DRAW A KAWAII CHARACTER ON DIFFERENT FABRIC WITH A TEXTILE MARKER TO MAKE A PATCH.

3. CUT THAT PATCH AND SEW IT ON YOUR T-SHIRT!

4. NOW YOU HAVE YOUR OWN ONE-OF-KIND KAWAII T-SHIRT LIKE LILICO!

PLAIN
T-SHIRT

KAWAII
PATCHES

LILICO IS SO CUTE IN HER KAWAII GRAPHIC T-SHIRT! SHE LIKES MIXING KAWAII AND CASUAL STYLE TOGETHER. I'M PLANNING TO MAKE AN ORIGINAL T-SHIRT FOR HER!

259

EMMA: 13 Years Old
HEIGHT: 5'4"
HOMETOWN: Brooklyn, NY
ZODIAC SIGN: Leo
FAVORITE FOOD: cheese pizza. It has to be thin crust!

FASHION DIY: EMMA!

1. FIND YOUR PARENT'S, BIG BROTHER'S, OR BIG SISTER'S SWEATSHIRT OR HOODIE. THIS SHOULD BE AN "OVERSIZE" TOP!

2. IF YOU WANT TO MAKE IT KAWAII, ADD SOME SMALL PINS TO DECORATE IT.

3. WEAR IT WITH LEGGINGS AND CHUNKY SNEAKERS!

EMMA'S FAVORITE STYLE IS L.A. SPORTY. IF YOU WANT TO DRESS LIKE HER, THIS OVERSIZE TOP IS A MUST-HAVE ITEM!

NALA: 13 Years Old (ALMOST 14!)
HEIGHT: 5'0"(CLOSE TO 5'1")
HOMETOWN: Brooklyn, NY
ZODIAC SIGN: Libra
FAVORITE FOOD: Pocky, Hi-Chew, and pickles!!!

FASHION DIY: NALA!

1. START WITH A PLAIN BLOUSE OR SHIRT.

2. FIND SOME OLD HAIR ACCESSORIES YOU DON'T WEAR ANYMORE.

3. CUT OFF SOME BOWS OR POM-POMS AND ATTACH THEM WITH SAFETY PINS!

4. YOU CAN PUT THEM AROUND THE COLLAR OR POCKET!

USE THIS PART!

I ADORE HARAJUKU KAWAII FASHION! I ALWAYS NEED TO HAVE SOME PINK ITEMS SOMEWHERE IN MY OUTFIT. THAT'S MY RULE!

261

HOW TO DRAW NICCO!!

DRAW ME!

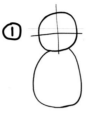

① DRAW
2 CIRCLES.

② DRAW EARS AND EYES.
INSIDE OF HIS EYES, ADD
WHITE BUBBLES AND
A BLACK BUBBLE.

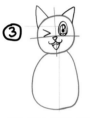

③ DRAW HIS NOSE
AND MOUTH. ADD
A TEETH LINE.

④ ADD LITTLE
CHEEKS.

⑤ ERASE CROSSED
LINES.

⑥ DRAW HIS ARMS.

⑦ THEN THE TOP
OF HIS LEGS.

⑧ FINISH THE REST
OF HIS LEGS.

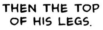

⑨ ONCE YOU DRAW HIS
TAIL, IT'S DONE!

MISAKO'S DRAWING TOOLS!

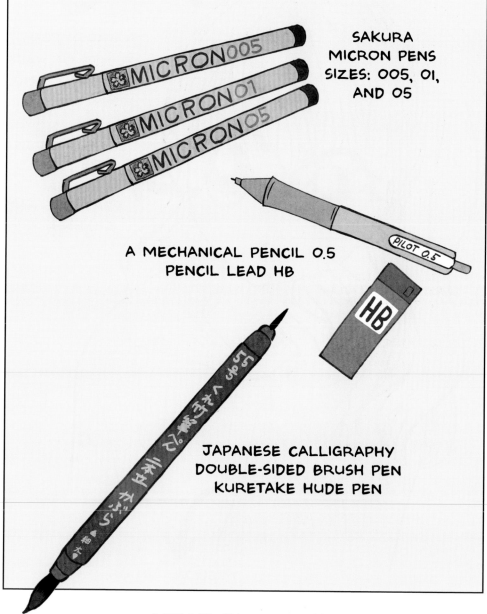

SAKURA MICRON PENS SIZES: 005, 01, AND 05

A MECHANICAL PENCIL 0.5 PENCIL LEAD HB

JAPANESE CALLIGRAPHY DOUBLE-SIDED BRUSH PEN KURETAKE HUDE PEN

LET ME SHOW YOU HOW I USE THEM...

A BRUSH PEN:

OUTLINES OF HAIR, FACE, BODY, AND CLOTHES

MICRON PEN 005 AND 01:

FACIAL FEATURES AND CHEEK LINES

MICRON PEN 05:

FABRIC WRINKLES

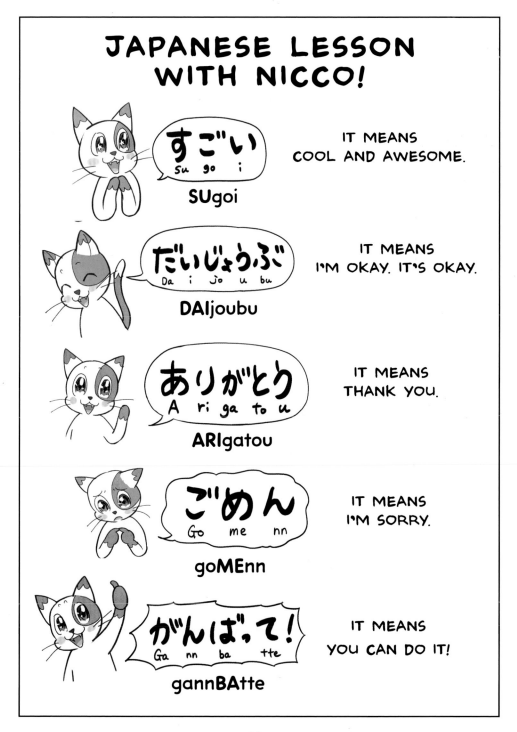

I was a proud baton girl!

ME

ME

This was my graduation day of elementary school.

Well, we are usually not allowed to smile for a school photo. I know it might be strange for you.

KONNICHIWA!

I'm a Japanese manga comic artist based in NYC.
Let me tell you, I'm still blown away by the fact
that I became an artist and live in America...
a country I'd dreamed of since I was just a kid in Japan!!!

I tried so many things and failed at so many things.
But I knew in my heart if I put my mind to it,
I could accomplish anything!

I started teaching manga at the Chapin School in NYC,
at museums and libraries, and with many private students.
After I got to know them better, they became my motivation.
Every kid has a story to tell. I want to make books that they
relate to. That's how the idea for *Bounce Back* was born!
I teamed up with my longtime friend/agent Janna Morishima.
We love the characters, the story, and most
importantly, my readers!

Besides making *Bounce Back*, I've been teaching
online manga lessons to kids who love kawaii manga
at my online community:

Learn Manga with Misako!

Find out more at www.misakorocks.com.

ARIGATO!

ACKNOWLEDGMENTS

SPECIAL THANKS TO...

Leyla Bayraktar as the model of Lilico
Luli Simonian as the model of Nala
Sofia
Mei

Feiwel & Friends, an imprint of Macmilan:
Jean Feiwel
Liz Szabla
Sharismar Rodriguez
Cindy De la cruz
Foyinsi Adegbonmire
The marketing team

My agent/longtime friend, Janna Morishima

My husband, Christopher

MY BETA READERS:

Patricia Ackerson
Max Aibel
Leyla Bayraktar
Eve Craven
Lauren Cummings
Rebekah Fertel
Deborah Garza Garcia
Laura Gonzalez-Ortiz
Naomi Hairston
Adriana Griffin
Anna Leventon
Sofia Liu
Kaitlyn Loo
Léonie Malihot
Julieta Mariano

Sam Masson
Karo Miller
Ceci Murray
Nina Murray
Jamar Nicholas
Ava Osmond
Joe Pascullo
Yesha Patel
Michael Plociniak
Luli Simonian
Monica Shah
Laurie Taylor
Caydee Yarbrough
Kathy Yang

My members of Learn Manga with Misako

Misako Rocks! subscribers

My students at the Chapin School
My students at the Hewitt School
My private manga students

Staff of Anime NYC
Brooklyn Public librarians
Staff of Copic Marker
Staff of the Dalton School
Staff of Gochi Gang
Staff of NY Comic Con

New York Public librarians
Staff of Teen Bookfest
by the Bay
Librarians who I got
to know at TLA

All the librarians who invited me to their awesome schools

My family and friends in Japan

My readers!!!

BYE BYE!

THANK YOU FOR READING THIS FEIWEL & FRIENDS BOOK.
THE FRIENDS WHO MADE BOUNCE BACK POSSIBLE ARE:

Jean Feiwel, Publisher
Liz Szabla, Associate Publisher
Rich Deas, Senior Creative Director
Holly West, Senior Editor
Anna Roberto, Senior Editor
Kat Brzozowski, Senior Editor
Dawn Ryan, Executive Managing Editor
Kim Waymer, Senior Production Manager
Erin Siu, Associate Editor
Emily Settle, Associate Editor
Foyinsi Adegbonmire, Associate Editor
Rachel Diebel, Assistant Editor
Sharismar Rodriguez, Senior Art Director
Cindy De La Cruz, Associate Designer
Mandy Veloso, Senior Production Editor

Follow us on Facebook or visit us online at mackids.com.
Our books are friends for life.

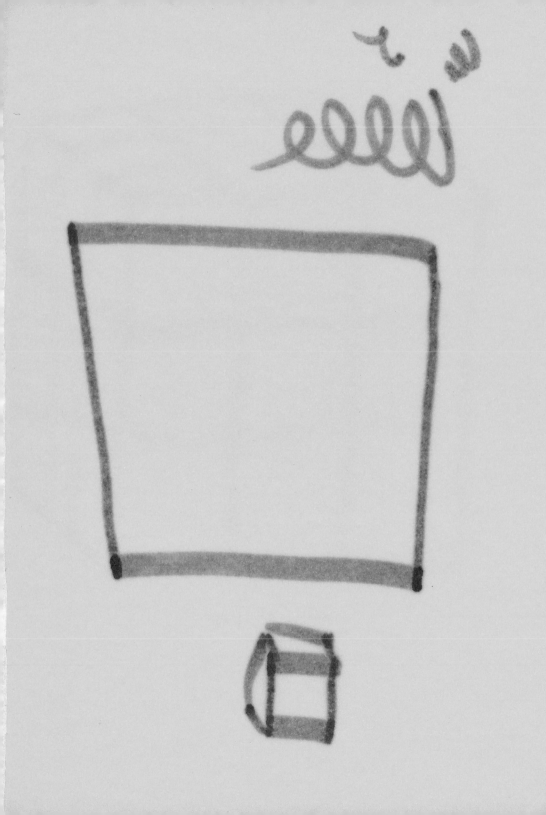